HORRiD HENRY
and the
Fangmangler

HORRiD HENRY
and the
Fangmangler

Francesca Simon
Illustrated by Tony Ross

Orion
Children's Books

ORION CHILDREN'S BOOKS

Horrid Henry and the Fangmangler first appeared in *Horrid Henry's Nits*
first published in Great Britain in 1997
by Orion Children's Books
This edition first published in Great Britain in 2016
by Hodder and Stoughton

1 3 5 7 9 10 8 6 4 2

A CIP catalogue record for this book
is available from the British Library.

ISBN 978 1 4440 1606 2

Printed and bound in China

The paper and board used in this book are from well-managed forests
and other responsible sources.

Orion Children's Books
An imprint of
Hachette Children's Group
Part of Hodder and Stoughton
Carmelite House
50 Victoria Embankment
London EC4Y 0DZ

An Hachette UK Company
www.hachette.co.uk

www.hachettechildrens.co.uk

For librarians everywhere

There are many more
Horrid Henry Early Reader books available.

For a complete list visit:
www.horridhenry.co.uk
or
www.orionchildrensbooks.co.uk

Contents

Chapter 1

Horrid Henry snatched his skeleton bank and tried to twist open the trap door. Mum was taking him to Toy Heaven tomorrow.

At last Henry would be able
to buy the toy of his dreams:
a Dungeon Drink kit. Ha ha ha –
the tricks he'd play on his family,
substituting their drinks for
Dungeon stinkers.

Best of all, Moody Margaret
would be green with envy. She
wanted a Dungeon Drink kit too,
but she didn't have any money.
He'd have one first, and no way
was Margaret ever going to
play with it.

Except for buying the occasional sweet and a few comics, Henry had been saving his money for weeks.

Perfect Peter peeked round the door. "I've saved £7.53," said Peter proudly, jingling his piggy bank. "More than enough to buy my nature kit. How much do you have?"

"Millions," said Henry.

"You do not," said Peter.
"Do you?"

Henry shook his bank.
A thin rattle came from within.

"That doesn't sound like millions,"
said Peter.

"That's because five pound notes
don't rattle, stupid," said Henry.

"Mum! Henry called me stupid,"
shrieked Peter.

"Stop being horrid, Henry!"
shouted Mum.

Horrid Henry gave the lid of his
bank a final yank and spilled the
contents on to the floor.
A single, solitary five pence coin
rolled out.
Henry's jaw dropped.

He grabbed the bank and fumbled
around inside.

It was empty.

Chapter 2

"I've been robbed!"
howled Horrid Henry.
"Where's my money?
Who stole my money?"

"What's all this fuss?" asked Mum.

"Peter stole my money!" screamed
Henry. He glared at his brother.
"Just wait until I get my hands on
you, you little thief, I'll –"

"No one stole your money, Henry," said Mum. "You've spent it all on sweets and comics."

"I have not!"
shrieked Henry.

Mum pointed at the enormous
pile of comics and sweet wrappers
littering the floor of Henry's
bedroom.

"What's all that then?"
asked Mum.

Horrid Henry stopped shrieking.
It was true.
He had spent all his pocket money
on comics and sweets.
He just hadn't noticed.
"It's not fair!" he screamed.

"I saved all *my* pocket money,
Mum," said Perfect Peter.
"After all, a penny saved is
a penny earned."

Mum smiled at him.
"Well done, Peter.

Henry, let this be a lesson to you."

"I can't wait to buy my nature kit,"
said Perfect Peter. "You should have
saved your money like I did, instead
of wasting it, Henry."

Henry growled and sprang at Peter.
He was an Indian warrior scalping
a settler.

"YOWWWW!" squealed Peter.

"Henry! Stop it!" shouted Mum.
"Say sorry to Peter."

"I'm not sorry!" screamed Henry.
"I want my money!"

"Any more nonsense from you,
young man, and we won't be going
to Toy Heaven," said Mum.

Henry scowled.
"I don't care," he muttered.
What was the point of going to
Toy Heaven if he couldn't buy
any toys?

Chapter 3

Horrid Henry lay on his bedroom
floor kicking sweet wrappers.
That Dungeon Drink kit cost £4.99.
He had to get some money by
tomorrow. The question was, how?

He could steal Peter's money.
That was tempting, as he knew the
secret place in Peter's cello case
where Peter hid his bank.

Wouldn't that be fun when Peter
discovered his money was gone?
Henry smiled.

On second thought, perhaps not.
Mum and Dad would be sure to
suspect Henry, especially if
he suddenly had money and
Peter didn't.

He could sell
some of his
comics
to Moody
Margaret.

"No!" shrieked Henry, clutching
his comics to his chest.

Not his precious comics.
There had to be another way.

Then Henry had a wonderful,
spectacular idea.
It was so superb that
he did a wild war dance for joy.

That Dungeon Drink kit was
as good as his.
And, better still, Peter would give
him all the money he needed.

Henry chortled.
This would be as easy as taking
sweets from a baby . . .
and a lot more fun.

Chapter 4

Horrid Henry strolled down the hall
to Peter's room.

Peter was having a meeting
of the Best Boys Club
(motto: Can I help?)
with his friends Tidy Ted, Spotless
Sam and Goody-Goody Gordon.

What luck. More money for him.

Henry smiled as he put his ear to
the keyhole and listened to them
discussing their good deeds.

"I helped an old lady cross the road and I ate all my vegetables," said Perfect Peter.

"I kept my room tidy all week," said Tidy Ted.

"I scrubbed the bath without being asked," said Spotless Sam.

"I never once forgot to say please and thank you," said Goody-Goody Gordon.

Henry pushed past the barricades
and burst into Peter's room.

"Password!"

screeched Perfect Peter.

"Vitamins,"

said Horrid Henry.

"How did you know?"
said Tidy Ted, staring open-mouthed
at Henry.

"Never you mind," said Henry, who was not a master spy for nothing.

"I don't suppose any of you know about Fangmanglers?"

The boys looked at one another.

"What are they?" asked Spotless Sam.

"Only the slimiest,
scariest,
most horrible and
frightening monsters
in the whole world," said Henry.
"And I know where to find one."

"Where?"
said Goody-Goody Gordon.

"I'm not going to tell you,"
said Horrid Henry.

"Oh please!" said Spotless Sam.

Henry shook his head
and lowered his voice.
"Fangmanglers only come out at
night," whispered Henry.
"They slip into the shadows then
sneak out and . . .

. . . **bite you!"**

he suddenly shrieked.

The Best Boys Club members
gasped with fright.

"I'm not scared," said Peter.
"And I've never heard of
a Fangmangler."

"That's because you're too young,"
said Henry. "Grown-ups don't
tell you about them because they
don't want to scare you."

"I want to see it," said Tidy Ted.

"Me too," said Spotless Sam and
Goody-Goody Gordon.

Peter hesitated for a moment.
"Is this a trick, Henry?"

"Of course not," said Henry.
"And just for that I won't let
you come."

"Oh please, Henry," said Peter.

Henry paused.
"All right," he said.
"We'll meet in the back garden
after dark. But it will cost you
two pounds each."

"Two pounds!" they squealed.

"Do you want to see a Fangmangler
or don't you?"

Perfect Peter exchanged
a look with his friends.
They all nodded.

"Good," said Horrid Henry.
"See you at six o'clock. And don't
forget to bring your money."

Tee hee, chortled Henry silently.
Eight pounds!
He could get a Dungeon Drink kit
and a Grisly Ghoul Grub Box
at this rate.

Chapter 5

Loud screams came from
next-door's garden.

"Give me back my spade!" came
Moody Margaret's bossy tones.

"You're so mean, Margaret,"
squealed Sour Susan's sulky voice.

"Well, I won't.
It's my turn to dig with it now."

WHACK!

THWACK!

"WAAAAAAA!"

Eight pounds is nice,
thought Horrid Henry,
but twelve is even nicer.

"What's going on?"
asked Horrid Henry, smirking as
he leapt over the wall.

"Go away, Henry!"
shouted Moody Margaret.

"Yeah, Henry," echoed Sour Susan,
wiping away her tears.
"We don't want you."

"All right," said Henry. "Then I won't tell you about the Fangmangler I've found."

"We don't want to know about it," said Margaret, turning her back on him.

"That's right," said Susan.

"Well then, don't blame me when
the Fangmangler sneaks over the wall
and rips you to pieces and chews up
your guts," said Horrid Henry.

He turned to go.
The girls looked at one another.

"Wait," ordered Margaret.

"Yeah?" said Henry.

"You don't
scare me,"
said Margaret.

"Prove it then,"
said Henry.

"How?" said Margaret.

"Be in my garden at six o'clock tonight and I'll show you the Fangmangler. But it will cost you two pounds each."

"Forget it," said Margaret. "Come on, Susan."

"Okay," said Henry quickly. "One pound each."

"No," said Margaret.

"And your money back if the Fangmangler doesn't scare you," said Henry.

Moody Margaret smiled.

"It's a deal," she said.

Chapter 6

When the coast was clear,
Horrid Henry crept into the bushes
and hid a bag containing his supplies:
an old, torn T-shirt, some filthy
trousers and a jumbo-sized bottle
of ketchup.

Then he sneaked back into the house
and waited for dark.

⁓

"Thank you, thank you, thank you,
thank you," said Horrid Henry,
collecting two pounds from each
member of the Best Boys Club.
Henry placed the money carefully
in his skeleton bank.
Boy, was he rich!

Moody Margaret and Sour Susan
handed over one pound each.
"Remember Henry, we get our
money back if we aren't scared,"
hissed Moody Margaret.

"Shut up, Margaret," said Henry.
"I'm risking my life and all you can
think about is money.

Now everyone, wait here, don't move and don't talk," he whispered. "We have to surprise the Fangmangler. If not . . ."

Henry paused and drew his fingers across his throat. "I'm a goner. I'm going off now to hunt for the monster. When I find him, and if it's safe, I'll whistle twice. Then everyone come, as quietly as you can. But be careful!"

Henry disappeared into the black
darkness of the garden.

For a long long moment
there was silence.

"This is stupid,"
said Moody Margaret.

Suddenly, a low, moaning growl
echoed through the moonless night.

"What was that?"
said Spotless Sam nervously.

"Henry? Are you all right, Henry?"
squeaked Perfect Peter.

The low moaning growl turned
into a snarl.

Thrash!

Crash!

"Help! Help! The Fangmangler's after me! Run for your lives!"

screamed Horrid Henry,
smashing through the bushes.
His T-shirt and trousers were torn.
There was blood everywhere.

The Best Boys Club screamed
and ran.

Sour Susan
screamed and ran.

Moody Margaret
screamed and ran.

Horrid Henry screamed and . . .
stopped.
He waited until he was alone.
Then Horrid Henry wiped some
ketchup from his face, clutched his
bank and did a war dance round the
garden, whooping with joy.

"Money! Money! Money! Money!
Money!" he squealed, leaping
and stomping. He danced and he
pranced, he twirled and he whirled.

He was so busy dancing and cackling he didn't notice a shadowy shape slip into the garden behind him.

Chapter 7

"Money! Money! Money!
Mine! Mine –" he broke off.
What was that noise?
Horrid Henry's throat tightened.

"Nah," he thought. "It's nothing."
Then suddenly . . .

. . . a dark shape leapt out of the
bushes and let out a thunderous roar.
Horrid Henry shrieked with terror.

He dropped his money and ran for his life. The Thing scooped up his bank and slithered over the wall.

Horrid Henry did not stop running
until he was safely in his room with
the door shut tight and barricaded.
His heart pounded.

There really is a Fangmangler,
he thought, trembling.
And now it's after me.

Horrid Henry hardly slept a wink.
He started awake at every
squeak and creak. He shook
and he shrieked. Henry had such
a bad night that he slept in
quite late the next morning,
tossing and turning.

FIZZ!

POP!

GURGLE!

BANG!

Henry jerked awake.
What was that? He peeked his
head out from under the duvet
and listened.

FIZZ!

POP!

GURGLE!

BANG!

Those fizzing and popping
noises seemed to be coming
from next door.

Henry ran to the window and
pulled open the curtains.

There was Moody Margaret
sitting beside a large Toy Heaven
bag. In front of her was . . .
a Dungeon Drink kit. She saw him,
smiled, and raised a glass of
bubbling black liquid.

"Want a Fangmangler drink, Henry?" asked Margaret sweetly.